A NOVEL

Just A Kid

A NOVEL

Just A Kid

RIE CHARLES

Red Deer Press

Published in the United States in 2020

Published in Canada by Red Deer Press,
195 Allstate Parkway, Markham, ON L3R 4T8

Published in the United States by Red Deer Press,
311 Washington Street, Brighton, MA 02135

Library and Archives Canada Cataloguing in Publication

Title: Just a kid / Ruth Charles.
Names: Charles, Rie, 1946- author.
Identifiers: Canadiana 20190158603 | ISBN 9780889955820 (softcover)
Classification: LCC PS8605.H36917 J87 2019 | DDC jC813/.6—dc23

Publisher Cataloging-in-Publication Data (U.S.)

Names: Charles, Ruth, author.
Title: Just a Kid / Ruth Charles.
Description: Markham, Ontario : Fitzhenry and Whiteside, 2019. | Summary:
"This contemporary and timely juvenile novel will help young readers learn about activism,
social and environmental responsibility and how to influence the adult world, even when it
seems no one wants to listen"-- Provided by publisher.
Identifiers: ISBN 978-0-88995-582-0 (paperback)
Subjects: LCSH: Children and the environment – Juvenile fiction. | Social action – Juvenile fiction. |
BISAC: JUVENILE FICTION / General.
Classification: LCC PZ7.C537Ju | DDC [F] – dc23

2 4 6 8 10 9 7 5 3 1

Red Deer Press acknowledges with thanks the Canada Council for the Arts and the Ontario Arts Council
for their support of our publishing program. We acknowledge the financial support of the Government of
Canada through the Canada Book Fund (CBF) for our publishing activities.

Edited for the Press by Peter Carver
Text and cover design by Tanya Montini
Printed in Canada by Houghton Boston

www.reddeerpress.com

For
Hazel and Shannon

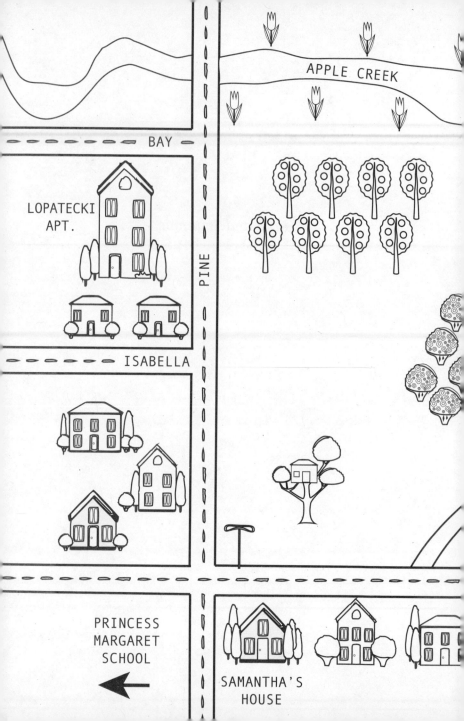

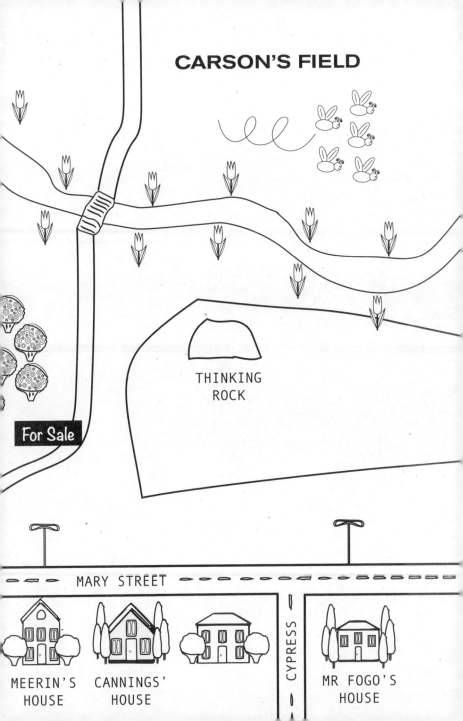

CHAPTER 1

A Field for Sale

"Oh, no. It can't be." Meerin's voice ran up and down and up again. "It just can't be."

She stared out the bedroom window. Her mouth opened but she didn't know what to say. Instead, she pulled strands of wispy black hair inside her cheek and sucked.

Every morning, rain or shine, school day or not, Meerin Hoy gazed out her window with a smile. Every single morning. But not this April morning. Yes, she ran across her room as usual. Yes, she yanked back the yellow polka-dot curtains as usual. But today there was no smile on her face.

"D ... a ... d! M ... u ... m!" Meerin bounded down the stairs, two at a time.

In the kitchen, Dad was stirring porridge on the stove.

Between stirs, he wiggled four-year-old Spencer into a sweatshirt.

"Dad, have you seen the signs across the street?" Meerin headed straight for the back door. She was still in her purple nightie covered with glow-in-the-dark stars.

"Where're you going, honey? You haven't had breakfast." The radio announced the 7:30 local news. "And you're not properly dressed ..."

"To Carson's Field." Meerin shoved her arms into the sleeves of her coat and stepped into her old running shoes. "There are two signs out there. I have to read them." In a whoosh of air, as the door opened and closed, she bolted outside. A fresh breeze blew her hair off her forehead. She heard Dad calling:

"Come back here, you two! Spence, you need long pants." But Meerin kept on running for the field.

Sure enough, there were two signs. One said FOR SALE in large red letters. However, Meerin and Spencer were staring at the other one. It was white with much smaller black print.

Dad joined them and peered at the sign as well.

"What does it mean, Dad? A zo-ning a-mend-ment?"

"It means the town wants to build houses here. In order to

do that, they have to change the law about how the land is used. So they applied for what's called a zoning amendment." Dad hopped Spencer into a pair of jeans.

"But what does it mean?" Meerin asked for a second time.

"When old Mr. Carson died, the town bought the land." Dad zipped up Spencer's matching jean jacket and lifted his son to his shoulders. "It was a farm then. I wasn't much bigger than Spence. The town must still have it zoned for farming, even though no one works the land anymore." He grabbed at Spencer's flying feet, one at a time, and pulled on socks. "Now, if someone wants to build houses here, the plan has to be changed from an area for farming to an area for houses."

"So we won't be able to play here? Like in the Ridley boys' fort?"

"I guess not."

"And Mr. Bothwell won't be able to take Tamara and Melissa fishing in the creek?"

"No, I don't suppose so."

"And Nana Tran won't be able to do Tai Chi here when she visits?" Meerin loved imagining the stork cooling its wings as her grandmother did her morning exercises in Carson's Field.

"You're right. She'll have to go somewhere else, I guess."

Spencer wriggled and bounced on Dad's shoulders.

"But wait, Dad, it says: *Submit comments to the Town Clerk by May 12.*" Meerin slid more long black strands of hair from the side of her face into the corner of her mouth. "So ... if someone doesn't want houses here, could they write to the town hall and say so? Maybe the people there might change their minds."

"I don't think anyone will do that." Dad shook his head. "Nobody ever objects or makes a fuss, especially over something so minor."

"But I object, Dad." Meerin put her hands on her hips. "And this is not minor. It's important. Where can any of us play? I *really* object."

A girl dashed up. "Meer, have you seen Annabelle?" It was Meerin's best friend, Samantha. Her pink sweatshirt was half pulled on, higgledy piggledy, one arm in, one arm out.

Meerin, Spencer, and their father all shook their heads.

"It's awful. She hasn't come for breakfast," Samantha gasped. "I've got to find her." She ran off in a flurry of arms and trailing shoe laces.

"This is even more awful," Meerin said to no one in particular. "Anyway, that cat's always going missing."

Meerin and Dad trudged back home, heads down, deep in thought. Spencer continued to bounce and wriggle on his father's shoulders. A smell of burnt porridge met them at the door.

"What in the world is going on?" said Mum as she upturned the porridge pot into the garbage. There were now bowls of shredded wheat, a jug of milk, and glasses of orange juice on the table.

"Mum, they're going to build houses across the street. It's terrible." Meerin scrunched up her face. "Where will me and the other kids play?"

"The other kids and I," muttered Dad, the school teacher as well as the father.

Mum untangled the damp hair from Meerin's cheek and mouth. "Hurry up now. We can talk about it after we sit down to breakfast."

Between slurps of juice and milky shredded wheat, Meerin told her mother about the signs.

"You're right," said Mum. "It would be a shame to develop Carson's Field. But no one will do anything. You'll see."

"But, Mum ... Dad, we have to stop it. Even adults use it, like Mr. Cannings and Mr. Jorgenson. And Mrs. Colleto won't be able take her Grade Fives there to study bugs and leaves and stuff." Meerin's eyes went from Mum to Dad and back again.

"That's enough for now. We've got to get moving. You'll be late for school."

Meerin screwed up her face. She was about to say something else, but Dad gave her one of his no-more-nonsense looks. She raced up the stairs.

"Heh! It's Annabelle," said Spencer. A large gray ball of fur poked her nose down from the top of the stairs. "How did she get in?" Spencer scooped up the cat and carried her down the stairs past the mini-aquarium to outside. "Just you stay away from Goldee and Fishee."

But Meerin didn't care about Annabelle. Or about Goldee or Fishee. She had an idea. Her unhappiness turned to excitement. A fantastic idea that would make the people at the town hall change their minds about Carson's Field. Easy as pie.

CHAPTER 2

The Petition

Saturday was cloudy with the shivery smell of spring rain in the air. Meerin drew back the curtains in her room. She hoped the signs weren't there. But of course they still were.

The afternoon before, in Samantha's basement, Meerin had explained her idea to her friend. "Remember Ms. Munro told us last fall about petitions?"

Samantha did a skip and a little twirl. "Yeah. Sort of. But I've forgotten. What's a petition?"

"You know. You put a bunch of words on a paper saying how something is really, really important. Then you get lots of other people to sign it who think so, too. When you're finished, you take it to the people in charge of whatever it is."

Samantha skipped and twirled again. Still, she looked doubtful.

"But I thought she said people did that on Facebook."

"She did. But she also said you can go door to door with paper and a pen. And we don't have Facebook." Meerin opened her eyes wide and beamed her beamiest smile. "Soooo, what I was wondering ... could we use your computer to write the words out? Then we could go door to door tomorrow. See, Mum has Simon Yanover for piano lessons now, and it's hard to think with all his plunking and mistakes and ..."

Meerin stopped. Samantha twirled again. This time she landed on the green swivel chair in front of her computer.

Together, the two girls typed out their ideas, one finger at a time. Of course they had to erase and find new words and check spellings. Finally, the petition read:

> We don't want Carson's Field to be changed
> for houses. It is a favorite place for all of us
> kids and parents and grandparents to play in.
> Please keep it the way it is.

It was eleven o'clock Saturday morning. Meerin and Samantha marched out of Meerin's house with two pens and several sheets of paper on a clipboard. "Bye, Mum. Bye, Dad," called Meerin. "Bye, honey," replied Dad from the kitchen. "Good luck. Have fun."

Piano sounds came from the living room. On a normal Saturday, Meerin liked to listen to Branden's piano lessons. She liked hearing his fingers dance, loud and soft, fast and slow. But today was not a normal Saturday. There were more important things to do.

The girls turned right on Mary Street. Spencer trailed behind on his tricycle. Mr. Cannings lived next door. He was the first to sign.

"Where will I go to do my birdwatching?" He twisted his binoculars hanging from a peg by the door.

"Don't worry, Mr. Cannings. This will stop it for sure. Abso-loodle-y."

There was no one home at the house on the corner, so they turned right again on Cypress. Mr. Fogo was watering a tiny patch of dirt. Meerin checked to see if the sky still looked like rain.

"Why are you watering the ground?"

Mr. Fogo lifted his gaze.

"I want to make sure this grass seed takes." An arc of water rose and spattered Spencer's trike. "It looks like Carson's Field is going to be full of houses soon. There'll be no more marbles there for me and my grandson, I reckon."

"Oh, yes, there will be." Meerin held out her clipboard. "Would you like to sign this, Mr. Fogo?"

He peered through the bottom of his glasses. "It's a sorry day when we have to fight to keep a nice piece of land just to muck about on." Then Mr. Fogo smiled. "Good for you, Meerin. Where's that pen of yours?"

Spencer zipped down the driveway in front of the girls.

"It's my turn to hold the clipboard." Samantha grabbed at the pens, too.

"Oh, and don't forget Mrs. Lopatecki. You know, that's the lady in the basement apartment on Bay Street." Mr. Fogo called after them. "When it's warm, she likes to read in Carson's Field."

Up John Street, down Cedar, and around on Isabella, it was much the same. Jeannie and Jennie's mum, Mrs. Chan, was sad. "I like to walk there with my girls. They love to pick the wild daisies. But, honestly, I'm not sure the people in charge are going to change their minds."

Mr. Jorgensen puffed and huffed when he heard the news.

"My thinking rock. What will happen to my thinking rock? That's where I go to get good ideas. And remember and dream."

Even Mrs. Coletto, with the too-busy-to-talk face, made time for Meerin when she heard of the housing development. "That's impossible. Where will I take my class for nature study?"

And in the middle of it all, Mikey McCann cycled by. "Whatcha doing, Meer ... Sam?"

Meerin explained about petitions and signing and changing the mayor's mind.

"Wait," he said. "So by signing this, we're going to stop all those houses? That's awesome." And of course he signed.

All weekend, sometimes with Spencer, sometimes without Spencer, the girls trailed up and down the streets. In between houses, Samantha hipped, hopped, and chattered.

"We're best friends, aren't we?"

Meerin nodded.

"You'll come to my dance recital, won't you, Meer?"

She nodded again.

"We'd better be in the same class together next year. I'd die if we weren't."

Again and again, Meerin nodded.

"Don't you love Ms. Munro? She reads the best stories."

But Meerin really wasn't listening. Mostly, she concentrated on who was not at home. Those places she would have to go back to later, because she wanted to get everybody, absolutely everybody, to sign.

On Sunday, even Annabelle the cat followed them all the way down Hickory Street. Samantha had to carry her home.

Only Mr. Malecki didn't sign. Meerin thought it was because he didn't understand her very well. He'd come from Poland a few years back. She heard about him from his granddaughter, Tina, when they did a project on the family in Grade 2.

Monday morning, Meerin brought the petition to school. "Good for you," said Ms. Munro. She handed it around to the other teachers in the staff room. By 4:00 PM, Meerin had six full pages of names. Even the kids in Mrs. Coletto's class signed.

"That will definitely change the mayor's mind. No problem-o," said Meerin to Mrs. Coletto.

"Oh, don't get your hopes up too high, dear. They seldom listen."

CHAPTER 3

The Meeting
at the Town Hall

"Please, is the mayor in?" Meerin spoke to an empty waiting area. The late afternoon sun shone golden rays through the long windows.

She heard a murmur of voices through the wall. A door, shiny with varnish and a brassy name plate *(A. Miller, Mayor)*, was open a crack. She pushed against it.

"Is the mayor here?" Meerin whispered into the space. Two men sat across the room behind a long table. The larger man was speaking.

"You don't understand. If more people lived here, more people would shop here." He swung around on his chair and stared out the window.

"I agree with you, Mr. Miller. Having more people would

be great." A woman with long dark brown hair and a red scarf round her neck sat with her back to Meerin. "But you hired me to look into what the new houses on Carson's Field would mean for the town. So I have to look at the cons as well as the pros."

"Fiddlesticks. There are no cons. Everyone will love it. And call me Arnold. No one calls me Mr. Miller." He turned back toward the oak windows. "Look over there at Harry's Hardware. Hardly anyone buys nails or shovels or buckets there anymore. And how do the Wells make a go of their cafe? The only thing people buy there is ice cream in the summer."

"Excuse me," said Meerin.

"That may be true, Mr. Miller ... uh, sorry ... Arnold. But I have to study both sides. That's my job. Like, finding out how much it will cost to put in sewers and sidewalks. And who will pay for those and the expansion of our school? Perhaps that will be too much for the town." She shuffled her papers.

"No, no, no." Arnold Miller joggled his large cheeks up and down. "Everybody will want it. And y'know, if there were more people here, more doctors would come to Appleton and deliver more babies, and the schools would need more teachers because of all the new children."

"Excuse me," said Meerin again, her voice louder this time.

"Eventually there'll be so many new families, we'll be trying to stop someone building a shopping mall by the highway." He chuckled.

Meerin felt her face redden in frustration. She raised her voice to almost a shout. "May I speak to the mayor, please?"

The large man blinked twice, then peered across the room at her. "I'm the mayor. I'm busy. Can't you see we're in a meeting?"

"I need to talk to you. I have a petition." Meerin stretched out her right arm, papers in hand. "It's about Carson's Field."

The thin man next to the mayor reached forward. "Leave it with me. I'm the Town Clerk." His hair was gray, his suit was gray. In Meerin's opinion, his face was gray, too.

She yanked back her arm and the papers with it. "Why can't I tell you about it?"

"Because we're busy and you are a little girl."

Meerin felt her face redden again.

"Do you have a name?" said the woman in the red scarf.

"Meerin. Meerin Hoy."

"Hi, Meerin. I'm Gillian McGuire. Maybe I can help."

Meerin knew a kind face when she saw one.

"Someone has to help us. We don't want the town to build on Carson's Field." She handed the lady her petition. "We like it the way it is."

Gillian raised one eyebrow as she flipped through the pages of names. Her right foot waggled up and down. "She's got quite a list here ... Arnold." She passed the papers across the table.

The mayor interrupted. "Enough of this. We have to be out of here by 5:00. This is not a place for a little girl. Someone show her out, please."

"There's a meeting on May the 6th if you have any questions," called the Town Clerk.

Meerin knew it was time to go.

At supper, she explained it all to her family. "It's not going to be easy-peasy. They didn't want to listen to me. I'm just a kid."

"You mean you walked straight in on the mayor's meeting?" Mum shook her head. "No wonder they didn't want to speak to you."

"Your mother's right. You shouldn't have done that," said Dad. "They did take the petition, though. That's something."

"So what do we do now?" Meerin's words trailed away.

They sat in silence, except for Goldee and Fishee. The fish swam round and round. And Spencer chewed his raw carrots, rabbit fashion, front teeth up and down, up and down.

Ddrrring! Meerin jumped at the sound of the telephone.

"It's for me. It's Sam." She cuddled the phone to her ear. "Hi Sam. What's up?"

"Hi, Meer. Guess what."

"Sorry, Sam. I can't guess."

"It's Annabelle. She's gone again. All night and all day." Meerin heard Samantha take in an anxious gulp of air. "After supper, could you help me look for her?"

"Sure."

"Thanks, Meer. Mum says if we can't find her by tomorrow morning, she'll put an ad in the newspaper. See yah."

"Bye." Meerin turned slowly back to the table. Dad pulled at his reddish golden beard as Mum poured herself a cup of tea.

"Ooohh." Meerin's eyes widened. "I know, I know." Her face broadened into a smile. "Why didn't I think of it? The newspaper. I can go to the newspaper."

Spencer went on chomping.

CHAPTER 4

The Appleton Spectator Helps Out

Tuesday after school, Meerin locked her bicycle and helmet to a pole in front of the office of the *Appleton Spectator*. Charging into the Town Hall the day before may not have been such a good idea. *But what else could I have done?* she thought. Today would be different.

As she headed for the door of the newspaper building, a girl, all alone, was mirrored in the tall windows. Meerin stared at herself, then tidied her hair, tucking it behind her ears. She wished Samantha could have come but, for Sam, Tuesdays meant ballet. Meerin checked for more wispy strands of hair. Today would just have to be different. Pulling back the screen door, then the wooden one, she peered inside. Two faces looked up.

"What can I do for you, young lady?" said a man with large

glasses and the dark shadow of a beard.

"Does anyone here know about Carson's Field?" asked Meerin. She hadn't really thought about what to say. Or even what she wanted. It just seemed a good idea to talk to people at the newspaper.

"Where's Carson's Field?" the man asked.

"Well, it's over there." Meerin pointed in the general direction of home. "It's a field where all of us play and do stuff. The mayor says the town's going to build lots of houses there. And me and my friends, we don't like it. So I got a petition signed by nearly everyone in the neighborhood to keep it the way it is. But the mayor won't listen and it's not fair."

The man shoved his glasses on top of his forehead, came from behind his desk, and thrust his hand out to Meerin. "Hi. I'm Jack Jennings, the editor of this fine newspaper, and this is my assistant, Farah Aziz." He pointed to the woman sitting at the other desk, who was pulling out another chair.

"Do you have a name, young lady?"

"Meerin Hoy," answered Meerin.

"Well, Meerin, I suggest you sit down and tell Ms. Aziz all about it." He turned to Farah. "I'm on my way over to the Carrier place. You hold the fort." He tilted his head in Meerin's direction and headed for the door. "Maybe there's a story in this."

Meerin drew her chair closer to Farah. "Do you have any ideas about what we can do?" she asked.

"First, tell me more about this Carson's Field and the problems you're having."

Meerin liked Farah's smile and the way she leaned across the desk toward her. So she explained about the field again. She explained about going around the neighborhood. And she explained about going to the Town Hall. In fact, she explained several times so Farah could write it all down.

"W... e ... l ... l," said Farah at last. She dragged the word out as if she was thinking hard. "Maybe you could write a letter to the editor."

"What's that?"

Farah opened a copy of the previous week's *Appleton Spectator* to page two.

"Dear Editor," she read. "Everyone loves my Bonnie. She's a cocker spaniel and well trained. There is no reason to keep her on a leash, especially in a park. She needs to run and get her exercise."

"But what if someone else's dog doesn't like Bonnie?"

"Good question," said Farah. "But people can write their opinions. You can do that, too. For example, you can complain about the mayor not wanting to speak to you."

"Would it help?" asked Meerin.

"It might. But if you want to get it in this week's paper, you'll have to hurry. Letters are due by six o'clock tonight."

"Oh, that's impossible."

"Well, there's always next week."

Meerin knew she could not wait that long. She turned to Farah again.

Farah leaned closer. "If we're quick ... why don't we do it right now? Although, it's unlikely the mayor will change his mind. But it's worth a try. That's for certain."

Together, they wrote a short letter on the computer. It ended by asking the mayor to meet with Meerin and other members of the community.

Mr. Jennings walked in the door as Meerin was signing and handing it to Farah. "You still here?"

"I'm leaving a letter to the editor with Farah. You'll print it in this week's paper, won't you?" With a smile, she turned on her heels. "Thanks. See yah."

The wooden door slammed behind her. And the screen did a double jump and bump after it. Meerin climbed on her bicycle and headed for Samantha's.

Now the mayor will listen to me, she thought. This time, for sure, for sure.

CHAPTER 5

Gillian McGuire's Suggestion

Thursday after school, Meerin pedaled downtown to the newspaper office, again by herself. Samantha didn't come because she was crazy worried about Annabelle and went straight home to look for the cat. With the last of her allowance, Meerin bought a copy of the *Appleton Spectator*.

"Fresh off the press, as they say. Or the printer." Farah handed her a neatly folded paper.

On the bench outside, Meerin spread it wide. Halfway down the front page was an article with the headline: "People Unhappy with Proposed Development." She read slowly and carefully. Some words were too big, but Mum or Dad would explain them later. It mentioned her name and the petition. That made her happy. And she was even happier because it did not say she had barged into the mayor's office.

Her own letter was right in the middle, at the top of page two. Meerin felt her ears warm just to read it.

> *Dear Editor,*
>
> *Last Monday I tried to give the mayor a petition, with lots of names of people who do not want houses built on Carson's Field. He didn't want to talk with me or listen to me. I would really like him to meet all of my neighbors so he can find out how much we like the field. I hope that is possible. Would you, Mr. Mayor?*
>
> *Thank you,*
>
> *Meerin Hoy*
>
> *Nine years old*

And just to the left of her letter was an editorial with the headline: "Should Carson's Field Be Developed?" It was amazing. Almost too much.

Meerin sucked hard on her strand of hair and read on. There was another letter about putting dogs on leashes and, on page six, she found Samantha's lost cat notice:

> *Large, long-haired gray cat answering to the name of Annabelle, lost in the area of Mary and Pine. Much loved family pet.*
>
> *Please contact 261-4231.*

Meerin had never read the newspaper much before. Sometimes there were write-ups about a school concert. Other times, it published poems or short stories from school kids. Like last year, Jenny wrote a story about her visit to the Toronto Zoo. Meerin had wondered why that one had got in and not hers about the problems of having a little brother. Or Kari's about a ghost in their house.

Meerin was far away, thinking of friends and ghosts and having little brothers. For the first time in quite a long while, she was not thinking about Carson's Field, when a voice said, "Aren't you the girl who came into the mayor's office on Monday?"

Meerin blinked and looked up. It was the woman with the red scarf. "Yes, I'm Meerin Hoy."

The woman said, "Do you remember me? I'm Gillian. May I sit down?"

Meerin moved the newspaper along the bench.

"May I tell you something?" Gillian did not wait for an answer. "It sounds like you're really against building houses on Carson's Field. You know, though, it will be hard to change the mayor's and the council's minds."

Meerin pointed to her letter in the newspaper. Gillian's foot danced up and down as she read. She flipped her long brown hair over her filmy red scarf.

"By the way, that was really great the way you came into the mayor's office. And you're only nine years old."

"Ten. Next month." Meerin could barely believe her ears. Gillian closed and folded the newspaper deliberately, and folded it again. It swished and crackled.

"Well, as I said, chances are they won't change their minds about the houses. BUT ..." Gillian seemed to say the word in capital letters, "... if you really, really don't want them there, you have to come up with another idea. A better idea."

"What do you mean?"

"The mayor wants to make this town grow. That's why he wants to build the houses. It's a good idea. He'll get his houses. But if you don't want that to happen on Carson's Field, you have to find another place that's just as good—or even better."

"How do you know so much?"

"I'm a planner," said Gillian. "The Town has hired our company to study what it would mean to have all those new houses. The soil, the roads, the increased traffic. Stuff like that. Even what it would mean for the stores. We try to look at the good side and the bad side. For everyone. And, we can look at other ideas, too." Gillian glanced around, then back at Meerin. "Where else could they put all those people?"

Meerin shook her head. How was she supposed to know? She lived on the east side of Appleton. She went to school on the east side of Appleton. She played with her friends on the east side of Appleton. She rarely went to the other side of Appleton. Meerin slipped more of the usual wispy strands of hair into her mouth. She quickly pulled them out again. This was in public, she remembered.

"Can't you change their minds?"

"Oh, no. I just write a report." Gillian flicked back her hair. "I'm paid to give advice. That's all. It's the mayor and the councilors who make the choice. Partly because of what I say ... that's true. But also because of public opinion."

Meerin slid the folded newspaper into her backpack and unlocked her helmet and bike. She felt her shoulders sag.

"But you are public opinion," added Gillian, stressing the word "you." "Make sure you go to the meeting on May 6. Bring all your friends and family. And, in the meantime, look for other places to put those houses."

Meerin pedaled home slowly, her head in a whirl and her shoulders a little less heavy. She knew what she had to do, at least what Gillian said she had to do. And she sort of understood why. But she wasn't sure how.

"Annabelle ... Annabelle's back!" Meerin was thinking so hard she almost bumped into Samantha running up the street. "A lady on Isabella," Sam gasped. "She saw the advertisement in the paper. I'm going to get Annabelle right now. Want to come?"

Meerin began pushing her bicycle beside Samantha down Pine Street. She had hope again. If the newspaper worked for finding Samantha's cat, it would work for her, too. Definitely.

CHAPTER 6

On the Lookout

"What's the point?" said Meerin. "Annabelle is always running away."

It was Sunday afternoon and the cat had gone again. Meerin and Sam had looked for her under every bush and up every tree in Carson's Field.

"What do you mean, what's the point?" Samantha scowled as she pulled bits of leaf and twig out of her sweater. "If she was your cat, you'd look for her, wouldn't you?"

"But why does she always run away, Sam? Maybe she wants to live somewhere else." Ooops. Meerin knew that didn't sound nice. She wished she hadn't said it.

"Are you saying she doesn't like me? Doesn't like her home? With me? In my house?" Sam's frown grew deeper. She stuck

RIE CHARLES

out her tongue at Meerin. "Some best friend you are."

Meerin hadn't meant to be rude. "Maybe she's being a Curious George ... or ... or she just likes wandering." She grabbed Samantha's hand. "It's only, I have more important things to think about right now."

"What could be more important than Annabelle?" A redness crept up Sam's usually pale face. "Yeah, I know. Carson's Field. The people at the town hall are not going to change their minds, Meer. That's what Mum says."

"But I talked to someone. She knows a lot and she said we've just got to find another place for those houses. Mum has no time to help. Dad has no time. And Mum says I can't wander all over town by myself. Will you come? Will you help me look for other places? Please? Please? We can go on our bikes."

It took some time to win Samantha over. But when Meerin suggested they make a bunch of lost cat flyers for the telephone poles, Sam finally agreed.

"Anyway," she said, "there's a big empty lot next to my dance studio."

"Why didn't you say so?" cried Meerin.

"Well, you didn't tell me that's what you wanted—until now."

The two girls headed up Hickory past the school and over the bridge. Meerin's backpack held a pad and pencil—and food, because she was always hungry. That meant the usual raisins, nuts, apples, cheese, crackers, and a full water bottle. Samantha brought a pile of papers with pictures of Annabelle and a ziplock bag of plastic tacks.

At every corner, they stopped to put up a flyer. Sometimes there were so many papers on the poles, they pulled off the old faded ones and stuffed them in a garbage bin. At Samantha's dance studio, they wrote down the address. At Conway and Russell, there was another abandoned-looking lot. Meerin wrote down that address, too. And another by the Catholic Church. She wrote: *Mayberry Road, east of St. Joe's.*

Uphill and downhill they went, and around every corner.

At last, they dropped their bikes on the ground and stretched out on a patch of tired-looking grass under a willow tree, and ate. Meerin's brain seemed to munch and crunch, too. She thought about what they had seen. But mostly about what they had not seen.

RIE CHARLES

"Maybe the mayor's right. Maybe Carson's Field is the only place. Everywhere else, there's only room for one house here, two houses there." She lay back against the tree trunk and gazed off into space, eyes unseeing.

"Yummy." Samantha chomped cheese on a thin wheat cracker. "Old-fort cheese. Why does my dad always buy the yucky gooey kind?"

Meerin sat up, grabbed another chunk of apple, then gazed off again. But this time, she looked over Samantha's shoulder, straight across the street.

"Could that be a place for people to live in?"

Samantha twisted around. "I wonder what it used to be."

What it was now, was a mess. There was a building, three stories high, with several boarded-over windows. The parking lot was rough and uneven. Dandelions poked their not-yet-yellow heads through every crack.

"Let's check it out."

The girls jumped on their bikes and circled the block. On the next street over, there was another building in a similar state. *Surely you could put lots of houses here*, thought Meerin. *Or you could fix these up to look all new and clean, like Nana*

Tran's place in Peterborough. And it's only three blocks from downtown. Meerin rode home, excited.

As they passed the school, Samantha yelled and pointed. "Look." She pedaled ahead in a whirr of wheels, jumped off, and jammed her kickstand into the ground. There was Annabelle. She swept the cat into her arms, then onto her shoulder. "Oh, Annabelle. We found you. You are the best cat."

Meerin felt cross all over again. It wasn't fair, she thought. Why was it so simple for Samantha? All she ever thought about was dancing and her silly cat. Why couldn't saving a field be just as simple?

CHAPTER 7

The Town Meeting

It was May 6, the night people could go to a meeting to ask questions about Carson's Field.

Meerin should have been excited but she wasn't. She didn't even feel like smiling.

The mayor had not called her after her letter to the editor. Mum and Dad said he cared about the town and her neighborhood. Did he really?

When she had asked about the closed-up buildings near downtown, Dad had said, "Oh, the old box factory and the scissors company? They went broke several years back. That area's for business, honey. They wouldn't put houses there."

And Mum had said, again and again, "Don't get your hopes up too high, love."

So Meerin didn't feel like smiling. But she still told herself to be hopeful. Tonight just had to be different. Since her letter had come out in the newspaper, many people had stopped her on the street.

"Congratulations, Meerin." Mr. Cannings shook her hand. "Thanks for what you're doing." Both a camera and binoculars hung from his neck.

"Good job, Meerin. We'll all be at that meeting, even my parents." That was one of the Ridley boys. She could never remember which was which.

"I really liked your letter to the editor, Meerin. I'll be there." Mrs. Lopatecki patted her on the head. Meerin squirmed inside but tried not to show it. She wanted the lady to come to the meeting.

But many of the people also scowled and added, "The mayor won't change his mind, though. You'll see."

So Meerin tried and tried to feel hopeful even when a little voice inside her said, *What if this doesn't work?* She forced herself to squeeze the what-ifs away.

Mr. Cordelli, the janitor, was putting out more chairs as Meerin and Dad hurried into the high school gym. The room was filling up with people very quickly and it was hard for them to find a seat. On stage with Mayor Miller, who looked formal in a white shirt and tie, were four other men. One was the Town Clerk Meerin remembered from her dreadful time at the town hall. There were also three women, including the Gillian person.

When everyone was seated, Mayor Miller cleared his throat. "Welcome, everyone. I'm pleased to see such a good turn-out. It's important that people have a say in what happens in our community. The more the better. I care about our town and I'm sure you do, too." He cleared his throat again, more loudly this time. Then he took a deep breath.

"We're here tonight to talk about building on Lot 10, Concession Road 3, now Mary Street, backing up to and crossing over Apple Creek to the north side. We received a large report from our consultants." He gave Gillian a quick nod. "Copies are here for you to peruse at your convenience. If you have any questions about the report, Ms. McGuire can help you."

"What does *peruse* mean, Dad?" asked Meerin.

"Look at," he whispered and went back to stroking his beard. Meerin felt very small in this large room filled with so many adults and so few kids.

Mayor Miller cleared his throat for a third time. Meerin wondered if it was sore. "Each one of you, I know, wants the best for our town. So let's have a good discussion. Shall we begin?"

First, a man with a tuft of a moustache on a weather-beaten face got up. He wore a heavy green jacket and held a soft round hat in his left hand.

"Hhh hmm." He cleared his throat, too, not in a loud harrumphing sort of way like the mayor, but in a nervous sort of way. "Mr. Mayor, most of the members of our Naturalists Club are here. We are worried about this development." There was careful clapping from several members of the audience. The man talked about needing different kinds of land for different kinds of plants and animals and birds. "Even more exciting, Mr. Cannings, who lives on Mary Street, has seen a pair of loggerhead shrikes. They are rare and have not been found around here for years. The north side of the creek is perfect for them, with that large open grassy area and low trees and shrubs. These birds need protection and they need this land kept just as it is, so they can rear their young and come back next year."

Meerin sat up straight. She poked Dad in the ribs. He stopped stroking his beard.

Mayor Miller cleared his throat again, even more loudly. Gillian McGuire's foot waggled back and forth.

"Thank you, Mr. Ferelli. But I do think houses for people come before nests for our feathered friends." He grinned.

Meerin slumped down in her chair. Gillian McGuire's foot waggled faster.

Mrs. Singh, the third grade teacher, spoke next and explained how many of the teachers at Princess Margaret Elementary took the children out on that field for science and art projects.

"My thinking rock is just the best place to get a good idea," added Mr. Jorgensen. "Maybe you could try it, Mr. Mayor."

Meerin sat up straighter. She got a little more excited, a little more hopeful, as more and more of the neighbors got up to speak.

But then it was the turn of business people.

"If we had more families, there would be more children in my daycare," sputtered Mrs. Enns.

"If there were more women here to work in my factory, I could make more shoes," said Mr. Leblanc.

"What about more men?" a voice piped up from the back.

And so it went on. There were questions about the traffic. And would there be a sidewalk on the north side of Mary Street?

All of a sudden, a woman stood up. She was way down at the front, and Meerin couldn't see who she was or what she looked like. "My name is Lavinia Chu. I study bees. Every year I come here—I didn't know it was called Carson's Field until this week—to check out an endangered bee called the Rusty Patch Bumblebee. Carson's Field has one of the last known populations of them." Meerin could hear a restless shuffling from the crowd. "Probably because there's a lovely patch of native thistle at the north end. If you build houses here, that thistle and other native flowers will be gone and this bee will be gone for sure." The woman sat down.

"We don't want bees, anyway. I don't want my children stung." It was another lady's voice this time.

Lavinia quickly stood back up. "Maybe you don't realize it, but we need bees. They and other insects are important to all of us. Not just to people like me who study them. They pollinate flowers in the biggest trees to the tiniest plants."

"But they still sting," said the same voice.

"She's right," said another.

"If we didn't have them, ma'am, sir, we wouldn't have most of our food, like fruit and the cereals you have for breakfast. I'm sure the apple growers around here know this. Anyway, bumblebees are slow moving and will only attack if they're threatened. Besides, it's just the females that sting." There were whistles and hoots and laughter from the audience.

"All right, all right, that's enough. Is there anyone else who wishes to speak?" It was the mayor. Meerin didn't know what to think. Except she knew she was getting tired, tired of the talk, and just plain tired.

There was a scramble of feet. She craned her neck toward the front of the room again. It was the McCann twins.

"And who are you, boys?" said the mayor.

"Calum McCann," said Calum. "We're wondering." He paused and gazed out at the audience. "If there's no Carson's Field, where will we go to play soccer or throw Frisbees or wrestle?"

"That's a good question. I'll have to think about it. But I think it's time to end this ..."

"But Mr. Mayor, you haven't heard from me," said Mikey. "I'm Mikey McCann, and I want to know where we'll go when Mum and Dad say we have to stop playing video games?"

"Another good question, Mike. Thank you. Thank you, boys. Now, off you go."

The mayor rose from his chair. "And, ladies and gentlemen, thank you, too, for coming. It's getting late. I think we've heard all points of view. I thank you for your opinions and I thank the town councilors for being here and listening. We will make a decision at one of our next council meetings." The people on stage shifted their chairs and began to rise.

Dad leaned into Meerin and whispered, "Do you want me to say something on your behalf, hon? It's not too late." Meerin shook her head. He stood up and took his daughter by the hand.

"Then, come on, Meerin. We've done all we can. Let's go home."

But she pulled her hand away. If Calum and Mikey could talk in front of everybody, so could she.

"Stop. Stop. Can't I have a turn?" Meerin ran, almost tumbled, down the aisle from the back of the room. "You haven't heard from me." She had never spoken in front of lots of people. And she had never spoken into a microphone. But that didn't stop her. Saving Carson's Field was too important.

"I'm Meerin Hoy," she began. A light flashed from Mr. Jennings's camera. "Mr. Mayor, I gave you a petition with a gazillion signatures on it. That shows how many people don't want houses on Carson's field."

"Yes, my dear, we know that. We will take all that into consideration. And now it's time ..."

"But ... but ... I also wrote a letter to the paper, asking you to meet with the people from our neighborhood. But you didn't answer." She gazed around at the crowd and realized she didn't feel nervous. "I think it's because I'm just a kid. Little kid or not, it's rude not to answer letters." She turned back to the Mayor. "Will you meet with us, Mr. Miller? Please?" The crowd rumbled.

"Well, my dear, that's exactly what we're doing now," said Mayor Miller.

Gillian McGuire spoke up. "Mr. Miller, her name is Meerin." The mayor's face flushed.

"I mean at the field," explained Meerin. "Where we can show you what it's really like."

"How about it, Arnold?" yelled someone from the crowd. The camera continued to flash at Meerin and the mayor.

"Well, of course, my dear ... uh, Meerin." The mayor turned to the stage. "I'm sure members of the council and I can meet with you. How about Saturday? Not this coming one, but the next, at ten o'clock in the morning." He checked his phone and looked over at the councilors. "The 14th."

Meerin nodded. "At the field?"

"Carson's Field it is."

CHAPTER 8

At Carson's Field

The front page of the newspaper that week had a large picture of Meerin talking with the mayor. Beside it was a long article, under the headline: "Mayor Bows to Nine-year-old's Demands." Meerin had twelve copies because almost half her class brought the paper to school for her.

Saturday, May 14, was sunny. Cool for the time of year, with a breeze. Meerin had on a new pair of jeans and the blue Fair Isle sweater Grandma Hoy had knit for her. Dad made her a breakfast of porridge, of course, with milk and brown sugar, then toast and honey and an orange.

At exactly 10:00 AM, Meerin saw five cars pulling up in front of their house. Others parked around the corner on Cypress.

The mayor stepped out of the first car. Behind him came other members of the council and, of course, Mr. Jennings and Farah Aziz from the *Appleton Spectator*.

The field swarmed with color and people and sound. Calum and Mikey McCann were throwing a Frisbee back and forth, back and forth, while Mr. Cannings chatted with three other men who peered through binoculars at the sky. Jennie and Jeannie dragged their mother across to Apple Creek, while Baby Kevin cried all the way in the carrier on Mrs. Chan's chest. Mr. Fogo, naturally, was playing marbles on a patch of sand with his grandson and two other children Meerin didn't know. And Mrs. Lopatecki and another lady pretended to read in their lawn chairs. Even Mrs. Colleto and her three children were there. Butterfly nets in hand, they swooped in and out and around and over the bushes. And Danny and the Ridley boys climbed to the tree-fort. The ancient apple tree danced with new green leaves and tight buds of pink blossoms.

Meanwhile, Spencer rode up and down, up and down and around, his helmet on backwards. And, of course, Samantha had Annabelle on a pink leash.

There were others from Isabella, Bay, and Cedar, people

Meerin knew from her door knocking—like George Zappa, who lounged against a lamppost, phone in hand, nose rings glinting in the sun. And others she didn't know. She was sure the field had never seen so many people at one time. Everyone was there. Everyone except Mr. Jorgensen. He was not on his thinking rock.

Meerin wondered why. And that wondering gave her an idea. She walked straight up to Mayor Miller, took him by the hand, and led him to a huge chunk of granite.

"This is where Mr. Jorgensen sits," she explained. "It's his thinking rock. Where he gets good ideas. Maybe you can get lots of good ideas here, too."

The mayor sat. He looked around at the running and climbing and swooping and marble playing. He watched the town councilors wander from group to group and talk with each in turn. Even with Danny, who was hanging from one of the branches above the tree-fort and talking to a woman in a woolly green coat. Her head bobbed.

And Meerin watched the Mayor.

"We definitely need those houses ... er ... Meerin." The mayor finally remembered her name.

"Aren't there other places for them? What about the Box

Factory and the Scissors Company? They're close to all the stores. My nana would love it there."

"But that area's for business."

"Why does it have to be for business?"

"Because it's always been for business." Mayor Miller pulled at his left ear, blinked, and stared off into the distance.

"Mind you," he said to no one in particular, "the water and sewer and roads are all built. But no ... we couldn't get twenty-three houses there."

He seemed to be arguing with himself. "Well, maybe if they were townhouses or ..."

Mayor Miller cupped his right fist under his chin and folded his left arm across his knees. "On the other hand, those buildings are rather special. Maybe we could renovate them for condos. But then, that wouldn't bring in families. No, that won't work."

Meerin looked around. The mayor was definitely not talking to her. Maybe he was talking to an imaginary Mr. Jorgensen. What should she do? She remembered her mother's words from a few months back, and now she understood.

"Sometimes," Mum had said, "sometimes, you just know the way you see it is the very best way. But people like to figure things out for themselves. You give them a nudge. Sure. But let them think they're the smart ones."

So Meerin nudged in a whispering sort of way. "Why couldn't there be a bit of this and a bit of that?" She pressed into his hand the list of empty lots she and Sam had found. "You know, a mixture." Then she stood very quietly. Very, very quietly.

Suddenly, Mayor Miller stood up and wiped the sand from his pants. "You're right, Meerin, this is indeed a good thinking rock. Please thank Mr. Jorgensen when you see him." As the mayor shook hands with Meerin and climbed into his car, Mr. Jennings's camera clicked and double-clicked.

"Drat," said Mr. Jennings. "I didn't get a word with him. I wonder if he'll change his mind. I wonder what the council will decide."

So did Meerin.

CHAPTER 9

Chicken Pox

For the next ten days, the ten days before the Town Council met to make their decision, Carson's Field seemed to be the only thing to talk about in Appleton. At least in east Appleton. And, despite the black flies and mosquitoes, many of those conversations took place in Carson's Field itself.

The story even made the local news on television. Meerin was unhappy the TV people didn't speak to her. But they did talk to Mrs. Coletto and Mr. Fogo, she reminded herself.

In addition, there were so many letters to the editor that the *Appleton Spectator* had to run two more pages than normal. Comments were both for and against. There was a letter from the owner of the pizza takeaway, almost pleading for the town to build more houses. And right beside the one from the Grade

6 class, listing all the reasons why they liked going to Carson's Field, there was one from a little girl. But Meerin knew it was really an adult who wrote:

Dear Editor:

My mum and I play "Pooh Sticks" in the creek. It's fun. Maybe the Mayor could play with us too.

Yours truly,

Marlene Imaba,

4 years old.

Even Mr. Jorgensen wrote in:

Dear Editor:

I was sad not to be able to go to the meeting at Carson's Field. I had the flu. I hear there were many people there. Now the Mayor and council must know how important the field is to us. But they and everybody else haven't heard from me. And for me, Carson's Field is very, very important because it contains my thinking rock.

You probably think it's just a big rock. It's much more than that. I get good ideas there. When my wife and I first moved here thirty-five years ago, that's where we got the idea to plant apple trees east of the town. My orchard did well. My son still grows good apples there.

I moved into town after my wife died. At my thinking rock, I remember all those years.

I also dream there of the future. For me, for my family, for the town. Thinking of the future, I think of Meerin Hoy. She is working to keep the field for all of us to play and dream in. She is a credit to her family, the school, and the community. Thank you, Meerin. Let's keep our special people and our special places.

Yours truly,

Harald Jorgensen

Meerin always liked Mr. Jorgensen because he treated her like a real person. But his letter was too much. It made her face hot just to read it.

Today was the day the Town Council was meeting to make their decision, and today Meerin's face was still hot. But not from reading Mr. Jorgensen's letter again. Of all the times, of all the days, Meerin was sick in bed with chicken pox. The fever had turned into ugly red spots on her belly and face and neck and throat and ears. She was hot, itchy, and cross all over.

"Oh, why? Oh, why? Oh, why?" she moaned. "Can you go to the Town Council meeting instead of me, Mum?"

"No, I can't, love. I don't want those houses built across the street any more than you do. And you must know I'd like to be at that meeting, and how proud I am of you for the all the work you've done. But I can't cancel piano lessons."

Meerin clung to her mother's waist, hair limp and damp and muddled.

"Anyway, someone needs to be here to look after you and Spence. Your father will go and he'll report back."

"Ooooh, I wish Sam could be here."

"I know, my love. But Samantha doesn't want to get sick before her dance recital."

Phooey on the dance recital, thought Meerin. She was wise

enough not to say it out loud.

That evening, the only way she could stop thinking about the meeting was to play with Spencer and his play-doh. Meerin punched and pounded. She rolled out people and squeezed the leftover bits into trees and cats. Soon the whole of Carson's Field came to life in her bedroom.

The phone rang. "It's bedtime for you, Spence," croaked Meerin and hurried into the kitchen as fast as her tired legs would let her.

"Hi, Sam."

"Hi, Meer. Guess what?"

"Yeah, I can guess. Annabelle ran away again. Don't you know there are bigger things to worry about tonight?" Meerin wanted to yell but her throat was too sore. "I'm tired and going back to bed. Bye." She jammed down the off button. "Annabelle. Shmannabelle. All she ever talks about is that silly cat."

The telephone rang.

"Hello ... oh, hiya, Sam ..."

"That was rude." Sam's voice yelled from the phone. "You didn't even listen. You're not my friend anymore."

Meerin opened her mouth to speak but heard a click and then empty air. She banged her hand on the counter. Fishee and Goldee bobbed and dived. Maybe I was rude, she thought to herself, but Sam didn't have to shout at me. She didn't even let me say sorry. Anyway, maybe I don't want her as a friend, either.

Meerin stomped back to bed. She wanted to yell and scream. At Mrs. Gray on the piano for stumbling and fumbling through Beethoven's *Sonatina in G*. At Annabelle for running away. At Samantha for not wanting to be her friend. Instead of yelling and screaming, she buried herself under her blankets and whispered, "Dad, come home, please. Come home now."

CHAPTER 10

The Council Decides

"There were so many people making so much noise, the council couldn't talk," explained Dad the next morning. "They finally closed the meeting to the public."

Meerin gave him a spotty stare. Eventually she pulled a strand of hair from her mouth.

"What's going to happen now?"

Dad shrugged his shoulders.

And that's how it stayed. The *Appleton Spectator's* headlines were: "Council Unable to Decide."

A week went by and Meerin was back at school. Her spots had faded but her oomph was gone. Was she still sick? Was it because Samantha wouldn't talk to her? Or was it the field? Had all her hard work and hope been for nothing? If she thought about Carson's Field, she was sad. And, of course, she thought about it. Of course she was sad.

Every morning at breakfast, Dad said, "No news is good news, honey. But you have to prepare yourself. Chances are ..."

"... they won't change their minds," finished Meerin in a dull voice.

Every morning Mum gave her an extra-squeezy hug and said, "Why don't you talk to Samantha, love. I'm sure she wants to play with you as much as you want to play with her."

But Meerin never did.

The following Saturday, as usual, Meerin dragged the curtains on her bedroom window back, like she was pulling a very heavy sliding door. As usual, at least, since that horrible day in April. And like that same day in April, she stared, pulling wispy bits of hair into her mouth.

"It's all over. It's finished," she said, in a grim and cloudy voice.

There was a new sign on Carson's Field. The old "For Sale" one was gone. The zoning amendment sign was gone, too. And she knew exactly what had happened, because she remembered what happened last year in Peterborough. There had been a big

"For Sale" sign on the mansion next door to Nana Tran's place. And the next time they came, there was another sign. It had a drawing of a humungous new building.

Meerin did not want to know how many houses were going to be on Carson's field, or what they would look like. She simply did not want to know.

She slid the strands of hair from her mouth and stuck them behind her ear. Hope was just like that piece of hair in her mouth, one moment comforting, the next yanked away and gone.

"It's all over. It's finished," her grim and cloudy voice repeated. All her hard work for nothing.

Meerin did not race downstairs. She did not scream out to her parents. No, she forced each leg into her jeans and each arm into a clean T-shirt. Then she stuffed her favorite purple nightie with the glow-in-the-dark stars under her pillow and yesterday's red turtleneck into the laundry basket. Next she wiggled into navy socks and bunched her hair up into a ponytail. Finally, she smoothed out her blankets and bedspread. It was time to go. She thumped down the stairs, one heavy step at a time.

In the kitchen, Mum and Dad sipped their coffee and talked above the radio. It blared out its regular Saturday morning broadcast. Spencer vroomed his truck between the table legs. Meerin tapped an itty-bitty bit of fish food in the water for Goldee and Fishee. It was something she did every other day.

"Good morning, love. You're up late." Mum poured a glass of milk for Meerin. Meerin reached for the Shreddies box. "And you seem a little pale." Mum felt her forehead. "Are you okay?"

"Mmm." She actually didn't know how she felt. Sad? Angry? Wanting to scream? Cry? And if she said anything about the new sign, would it make what had happened too real. So she changed the subject. "What smells so yummy?"

"Carrot muffins." Dad glanced at the timer. "They'll be out in five minutes. Want one, honey?"

"Yes, please." Meerin slopped freshly stewed rhubarb over her cereal. "Stop bumping into my legs, Spence. Just stop it." She kicked her foot out at him under the table. "What's up today?"

"The usual. Your mother's piano students, shopping, housework. And, oh ... Lin?" He turned to his wife. "Do you want me to pick up some tomato plants?"

"Good idea, and a chili pepper or two, please." The front doorbell rang. Mum got up, coffee in hand. She returned in a minute, her eyebrows raised in surprise. "It's for you, Meerin."

Behind her was the mayor, his red shirt open at the collar.

"Good morning, everyone," Mr. Miller boomed with a wide, friendly smile. He nodded to Dad, who was pulling the muffins out of the oven. "It's a gorgeous day out there. I have something to show you, Meerin."

Meerin did not smile back. "I know. The sign. I saw it. You've sold the land."

"Just come with me," said the mayor. Spencer vroomed his truck past them out the door. Mum and Dad followed.

Carson's Field was no longer empty. The Ridley boys did wheelies in the sand and Danny draped himself from the apple tree. Pale pink blossoms drifted down. The whole town council was there, too, even the lady with the green coat. And Meerin would recognize Gillian McGuire anywhere by her red scarf. Mr. Cannings hurried across Mary Street, binoculars in his hand. And Mr. Jennings and Farah Aziz both held cameras in theirs. But no one was looking at the sign. Or even at the deep purple lilac bush behind it. They were looking in the direction of the mayor, of Meerin's house, of Meerin.

Samantha bounded up with a big grin. "Isn't it exciting?"

Meerin almost said, *You've found Annabelle, right?* But she smiled instead. Sam was finally talking to her. Everyone else had grins, too.

Mr. Jennings pumped her hand.

"Well, how does it feel, Meerin?"

Farah Aziz pushed Meerin over next to the mayor. "Hold it." The camera clicked. "Again." She gestured to the right. "Over here, so we can get you with the sign." Click. Click. Click.

The sign was definitely different—green and gold with bold black printing. Out of the corner of her eye, Meerin saw a TV van lurch to a stop. Two men jumped out, one hoisting a camera to his shoulder.

"What does the sign say, Meer?" Spencer pulled at her sleeve. "What does the sign say?"

Meerin read it out loud, slowly, carefully.

"Meerin's Natural Park: For Meerin Hoy, who reminded us we need a place to think and just be." She stared down at Spencer. "I don't believe it."

Spencer squeezed her hand and stared back. "What does it mean, Meer?"

She looked to her left and to her right for Mum and Dad.

"Does it mean what I think it means?"

Dad scooped her up and swung her around in a circle as big as his smile. "It sure does, honey."

Mum joined them in another hug. "You are an amazing daughter." They read the sign out loud two more times, all together.

"I don't believe it," Meerin said again, shaking her head. "A park named after me. And I'm just a kid."

The mayor cleared his throat. "Ladies and gentlemen."

The television cameras rolled; fancy cameras clicked. The crowd bumped and poked its way to the sign, while town councilors tied red and green and purple helium-filled balloons to the wrists of little children. Mr. Cannings shook Meerin's hand. Mr. Jorgensen did, too. Then Mrs. Colleto and Mr. Bothwell hugged and patted her on the back. Phones on camera mode waved and bobbed and danced in everyone's hands.

"Ladies and gentlemen." The mayor cleared his throat again in his harrumphing sort of way.

Gillian McGuire pushed into the circle. "Way to go, girl."

Calum and Mikey McCann, because they were twins and did

everything twice, chanted, "Meerin ... Meerin ... Meerin ... Meerin!"

Mr. Fogo and Mrs. Lopatecki, walking hand in hand, thanked Meerin with a kiss on each cheek and said, "We knew you could do it, darling."

Then Jeannie Chan burst up to her with a bouquet of lilacs. "For you from Mummy's garden," she said.

"Ladies and gentlemen." The mayor cleared his throat for the third time. Then he shouted, "Let's just forget my speech and declare open the first new park in Appleton since 1967, named in honor of Meerin Hoy!"

Everyone whistled and clapped and shouted, "Yea, Meerin!" And whistled some more, as balloons danced in the morning sunshine. A red one flew up and away in the excitement.

"But what about the houses?" shouted a voice.

"We'll figure that out. My idea of a few here and a few there and a few everywhere else is much better. And the council agrees."

Eventually the television camera van drove away. Eventually the mayor and town councilors drove away, too. As the neighbors headed for home, Samantha walked up to Meerin with a shy smile.

"You're still my best friend, aren't you, Meer?"

Meerin nodded.

"Then, can I show you something?"

Taking her by the hand, Samantha steered Meerin in the direction of her house. As she opened the screen door, she paused and smiled at Meerin in a secret sort of way, then led her to the far back corner of the porch beyond the old couch. There, curled up in a wide wicker basket, was Annabelle with five tiny balls of gray and orange fluff.

"Aaahhh, kittens," whispered Meerin.

"That's what I tried to tell you," said Sam.

Meerin laid her flowers by the basket and stroked a purring Annabelle. "Can I hold one?" she asked Sam, as she cupped her hands under a small orange ball of fur.

"If Annabelle agrees."

Lifting each kitten in turn, Meerin inspected it from its tiny ears to its almost as tiny tail. "Look, this one has its eyes open. And they're blue." She put the last one down and gave Annabelle a long, lingering pat. "Thanks, Annabelle. You have lovely babies."

Meerin picked up her flowers and stood. She gathered any hair that had strayed from her ponytail and curled it behind her ears. Then she took a deep breath. "Sorry, Sam. I should have listened when you phoned that time."

"Oh, forget it, Meer."

"No, I mean it. A kid has to listen, too."

"It's okay. It's over." Samantha pulled her by the shoulder. "Come on. Let's go back outside and play—in your park."

"Good idea. Let's. But ... but wait ... maybe we can find a bumble bee."

Sam screwed up her face halfway between a "yea" and an "eek."

Meerin laughed.

"Oh, Sam, you're funny. And my best friend." They dashed outside and down the porch steps, two at a time. "Anyway, it's not my park. It's everybody's park. For ever and ever."

Acknowledgments

I am very grateful to Peter Carver of Red Deer Press for liking and believing in Meerin, and I feel very lucky to have such a marvelous editor.

A general "Thank you" goes to my new writing group. While Julie, Florida, and Bill had nothing to do specifically with this book, they had everything to do with my continuing to write.

I am also grateful for my partner, Rick, who listens patiently to my dithering over a particular word choice, or watches me wander in circles, wondering where my characters will go next in their journey. As well, I thank the staff at my local library who uncomplainingly bring in books from distance sources, saying: "It's just my job."

Specific to this manuscript, I wish to thank Lincoln Best for his bee information, my cousin Syd for the helpful bird ideas, and Sally McIntyre for her advice about planners. There are others who helped in perhaps smaller but important ways—they know what they did—Liz Campbell, Amanda Gray, my sister Jeannie, and Roger and Elizabeth Williams. I hope I have not forgotten someone.

Most importantly, I wish to thank the late Hazel Street Cannings and her granddaughter, Shannon, for inspiring this book.

Interview with Rie Charles

What made you want to write this story?

Many of us, both adults and young people, feel helpless in the face of the daily news crises around the world and about climate change in particular. It is easy to give up and do nothing. Few of us will become heads of government or attain some other high position of power. However, we can make changes in our own community, by our own actions, however big or small. And those all add up. I wanted to show a young person's determination to make a difference in the world and give us hope by her success. Meerin can be a model for others.

Why do you think the mayor ignores Meerin, first of all?

For several reasons. Meerin did not follow the normal adult

route of making an appointment to see the mayor and so the mayor probably is a bit put out. Plus he is busy in a meeting and sees interruptions as wasting his time. But I think the mayor is also one of those adults who normally do not listen to young people. In his case, it is possibly made worse because young people are not yet voters. He also seems to have a strain of self-importance in him. You notice he is somewhat disrespectful of Meerin by not remembering her name, despite several reminders. Because she is just a kid?

Other people don't ignore her—how do you explain the difference?

Most of the other people know Meerin personally, at least to some degree—they are neighbors, teachers at her school, friends. Farah and Mr. Jennings listen because, as reporters, it is their job to find out the concerns of people in the town.

What do you know of young people who, like Meerin, have spoken up and changed things?

I have not personally met any of these young people. I have occasionally read about them on the Internet and in the newspaper. One example is Greta Thunberg who refused to go to school as a means of drawing attention to the climate crisis. Her actions sparked a worldwide movement of young people to protest governmental inaction around climate change. Young people can and do speak up.

These days, do you think young people have the sort of community awareness that Meerin has?

Some do, some don't. Meerin's actions grew out of the possibility of losing something very important to her. Her awareness grew the more she became engaged. If the field had been on the other side of town, would she have been so passionate? I don't think so. If her parents and teachers had not been relatively supportive, would she have accomplished what she did? I don't think so. I feel, in general, all people have varying degrees of community awareness, but, for young people, the nature and focus is stimulated and increased by the actions and interests of parents, teachers, and friends. Adults model local and wider community awareness.

Why did you want to include Samantha as a character in this story?

As a writer, I wanted a friend of Meerin's age but with contrasting qualities within that friendship. The interactions between them allowed me to generate problems and interest. It also gave me a chance, for example, to show Meerin in not such a good light when she was sick, short-tempered, and rude. We all have our moments. So it then gave me the opportunity to show her realizing her mistake and apologizing.

In addition, *Just a Kid* is not only about saving land from development. It is also a story of community. And community starts with friends and friendships.

Why do you think it is important that adults listen to the opinions of young people?

Why not? Anyone can learn from anyone. But often we adults, in our supposed wisdom, think we know better just because we are adults. Because of our longer and wider experience, it may be partly true. But young people can and do have fresh ideas and energy, see the world in new ways, uncluttered by our longer histories, and can comment and ask questions that have profound implications for all of us.

Why are lots of the adults in the story willing to sign the petition and support Meerin's idea, but negative about the probable outcome?

Some of it speaks to the adults' history of their own unsuccessful attempts to make change. Some of it is trying to be protective of Meerin, so that she is not disappointed if her plans don't work out. Some of it is a general cynicism. Adults can put down the possibility of change, but, underneath, the words may serve to cover over their own felt responsibility or justify their lack of action to struggle for change.

Was there anything about this story that made it difficult to write?

Finding Meerin's age and voice. I first wrote this story for a younger age group and, therefore, with Meerin younger. Then I wrote it for this age group; then for an older one. But I returned to Meerin being nine, almost ten. I can remember the exhilaration at that age, of having a wide awareness of the world, and being full of hope and dreams and daring. The strong negative messages of being told "it" wasn't possible came, unfortunately, only too soon.

What is your advice to young readers who have important issues they want to speak up about?

Be brave. Speak up. Talk about it. Be persistent. And if you're respectful, you will be respected back. This time, on this issue, you may not be as successful as you dreamed. The important thing is that you tried. You will have gained experience and wisdom for the next time. Keep dreaming. And keep trying.

Thank you, Rie, for the inspiration.